years before giving up teaching to write full-time. At the last count she had written over 70 books.

She writes both fiction and non-fiction, but at present is concentrating on fiction for older readers.

Helen also runs writing workshops for children and courses for teachers in both primary and secondary schools.

How many have you read?

Who's Who?

Helen Orme

Rans⚫m

Who's Who?

by Helen Orme
Illustrated by Cathy Brett
Cover by Anna Torborg

Published by Ransom Publishing Ltd.
51 Southgate Street, Winchester, Hants. SO23 9EH
www.ransom.co.uk

ISBN   978 184167 687 6

First published in 2007

Meet the Sisters ...

Siti and her friends are really close. So close she calls them her Sisters. They've been mates for ever, and most of the time they are closer than her real family.

Siti is the leader — the one who always knows what to do — but Kelly, Lu, Donna and Rachel have their own lives to lead as well.

Still, there's no one you can talk to, no one you can rely on, like your best mates. Right?

1

A great idea

"What about a sponsored silence?" suggested Rachel.

"No – loads of people will suggest that. We want something really different."

"How about a sponsored silence for teachers? That would be different!"

Siti made a rude noise.

"A dress down day?"

"Too childish!" Siti was getting cross with herself. She needed a really good idea.

It was activities week at school so, for once, the Sisters were split up. The Sisters were Siti's friends. They had been mates since they were really small and did everything together.

Rachel and Siti had decided to do work in the community.

There were lots of things planned for the week, like visiting the hospital, spending an afternoon with some senior citizens showing them how to surf the net, and working at a playgroup for disabled children.

The group had been asked to come up with some fundraising ideas. Whoever came up with the best idea could give all the money they raised to the charity of their choice.

"I know – we could run a crèche in the shopping centre," said Siti. "I bet loads of the parents would pay to get us to look after their little ones."

They were really pleased when Miss Drake chose their idea.

"It might take a bit of setting up," she said. "But I'm sure I can do it."

2

All sorted

Siti and Rachel had had a great week. The playgroup had been the best.

"I really like working with the little ones," said Rachel.

"Yeah, so do I, but I like the older ones better than the babies," agreed Siti.

Rachel laughed. "You couldn't tell one baby from another," she said.

"It was all right if they were wearing different clothes, but most of the time they all look the same."

On Thursday, Miss Drake came to talk to them.

11

"I've got it all sorted," she said. "We can have space in the shopping centre, near the food hall."

"Good," said Siti. "Lots of cups of coffee!"

"I shall want you there nice and early," said Miss Drake. "We've got lots to get ready."

"Who else is coming to help?" asked Rachel.

"Well, I've asked Miss Giles, and I hope that lots of your group will come along as well."

Siti pulled a face, but was careful not to let Miss Drake see.

Miss Drake went off to find some others from the group.

"What on Earth did she ask Miss Giles for?" said Siti. "She's totally useless!"

"Yeah, but she's nice," said Rachel.

"I know she's nice, but she forgets everything you tell her."

"But she's only going to be helping. Miss Drake will sort it all. Don't worry about it."

3

The shopping centre

Siti and Rachel arrived at school early the next morning.

"What can we do to help?" Siti asked Miss Drake.

"You two go to the shopping centre with Miss Giles. You can start setting everything up."

Miss Giles took them to the shopping centre in her car. They went to look for the centre manager. Soon, they were upstairs in the food hall.

The manager showed them a roped off area.

"You're close to the toilets here," he said. "That should help with the little ones."

Siti laughed. She had younger brothers and sisters and knew all about toilet trips.

"You're near to the lifts too, so you should catch the mums and dads when they come up from the car park."

"I've got some posters," said Miss Giles, unrolling some sheets of paper. "Go and put one up near the lifts, one at the top of the stairs and we'll put one here, too."

Siti and Rachel went off to put up the posters.

"See," said Rachel. "She's O.K."

They got back to their area. Miss Giles had bought them both cups of coffee. She was busy putting up tables and making a ring inside the ropes.

"We've got to make sure the little ones can't get out," she said. "We'll put chairs round as well."

She pulled at the nearest table – and the coffee cups fell to the floor.

"Ow!" said Siti, as the hot coffee went all over her.

Miss Giles started to flap. She pulled a wad of tissues from her pocket. She moved towards Siti to give them to her. But she hadn't seen the puddle of coffee on the floor. She slipped and fell into it.

Siti looked at Rachel and shook her head.

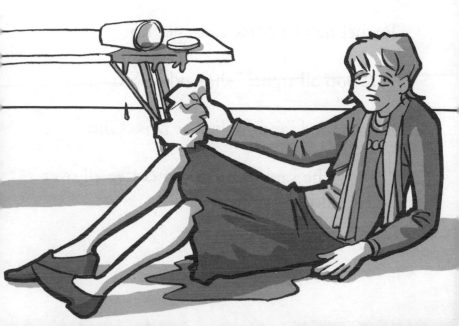

4

Everything under control

Rachel helped Miss Giles get up.

"Are you all right?" she said to Siti.

Siti nodded, and looked at Miss Giles.

"Miss," she said, "you've got coffee all over your backside."

Miss Giles twisted round to look.

"Oh dear," she said.

"You go and get clean and I'll clean up the mess," said Rachel.

By the time Miss Giles came back, everything was sorted out and the tables and chairs had been put in place.

Just then, Miss Drake arrived with Sally, Gill, Frankie and Hannah.

"Aziz and Pete are coming on the bus," she said. "They'll be here later. You look as if you've got everything under control here."

Siti smiled at the others, "Yeah, we're fine," she said.

"Where have you put the boxes?" Miss Drake looked at Miss Giles.

"Oh no! I forgot to put them in the car."

"You'll have to go back to school and get them," Miss Drake sighed loudly. "You were supposed to be bringing the toys."

Miss Drake started to get things organised. Sally and Gill were to take the money, Frankie and Hannah were to look after the toddlers with the boys to help, when they arrived, and Siti and Rachel were to look after the babies.

5

"Do something about the babies!"

It was quiet to begin with, but by ten o'clock they were getting more and more people. Luckily, Miss Giles had got back with the toys, and Pete and Aziz had arrived too.

Pete had started a football game with some of the older ones. They were having a great time.

Siti and Rachel were having it easy, as most of the babies were sleeping. Siti had pinned a mobile phone number to each of the buggies. She wasn't going to have anything to do with screaming babies if she could help it!

Then, suddenly, it all went wrong!

It wasn't really Miss Giles' fault. She was just in the wrong place at the wrong time.

The problem with little children, as Miss Drake said afterwards, is that they need lots and lots of 'stuff'. The 'stuff' came in bags, and the bags got scattered all round.

Miss Giles was walking across the area when Aziz kicked the football. It wasn't his fault either. It wasn't as if it had been a hard kick. Miss Giles tried to get out of the way, and tripped over someone's bag. That would have been O.K., but she crashed into one of the chairs and hit her head.

Sally screamed and Gill rushed over to help. Then the toddlers started to join in.

The noise was awful!

Lots of the toddlers had begun to howl loudly. That started off two of the babies.

Miss Drake soon got everything sorted out. She wouldn't let Miss Giles get up.

"Aziz," she said, "go and get the first aid people."

"Siti, can you and Rachel do something about those babies, please."

6

The wrong one

It was chaos! Mums and dads came rushing back to the creche to claim their children.

Siti picked up one of the babies. Rachel picked up another and rocked it.

"Rachel," called Miss Drake, "quick, can you get that little one – he's trying to escape."

Rachel pushed her baby into Siti's arms and rushed off to help.

Siti put the quiet baby back in its buggy.
She cuddled the other one and then put that
down too.

Two mums arrived. They were loaded with bags. One grabbed a screaming toddler and the other took one of the buggies. They hurried away quickly and headed towards the coffee shop.

Soon it was quiet again. Lots of the children had gone. Miss Giles had been taken away by the first aiders.

Another mum arrived. She collected the buggy and bent over to tidy the covers.

"That's not my baby! What have you done with my baby?" she demanded, looking around wildly.

Siti thought fast. There had only been two buggies. She looked round and saw the other mum pushing her buggy towards the lift.

She couldn't get to the entrance. There were people in the way and she had to act fast!

She jumped over the tables, pushed under the ropes and ran as fast as she could. She got her foot in the lift door just in time.

"That's not your baby," she gasped. "Sorry – it's the wrong one."

The mum glared at Siti but looked at the little object.

"Where's my baby? What have you done with my baby?"

"It's O.K. He's safe. Come back with me."

It was the end of the day. Everything had been sorted out, everyone had got the right child and they'd even made money.

Rachel and Siti decided to give the money to the playgroup.

Miss Drake looked at Siti.

"Next time you have a good idea," she said, "suggest it to someone else!"